This book belongs to:

....

EDSEL EDGAR EUGENE

THE MONKEY WITH NO NAME

by SUNNY GRIFFIN
ILLUSTRATED BY R.M. KOLDING

LANDOLL
Ashland, Ohio 44805

Edsel Edgar Eugene was a
very smart little monkey it did seem.

He grew up in a jungle that was
all luscious and green.

Deep into the jungle he would
go every day.

He was so smart not once
did he lose his way.

The gorilla said,
"Oh! If I only knew.

If you didn't have a name,
you'd be sad too.

I can't tell anyone who I am...

but what do you think
of the name Big Hairy Sam?"

Edsel Edgar Eugene thought for
a moment then quickly he said,

"With a name like that to the
alligators you're sure to be fed.

My name is so long,
with you I will share...

I'll give you 'Eugene,'
that's more than fair."

I just know I can make lots of
new friends...

now that I have a name, they will all
come out of their dens."

So off into the jungle the two did go.

But it wasn't long until they heard
a loud voice crying no, no, no.

They peeked through the bushes
and there they did see...

a big fluffy lion completely down
on one knee.

"I really need a name...
let me tell you why."

He lifted up his big wooly head
and said to them with a sigh,

"My friends won't let me be the
jungle king...

because I have no name for all
of them to sing."

The lion now called Edgar was as thrilled as he could be.

So going into the deep jungle now there were three.

As the three marched down the
path in perfect time...

they met an elephant who really
didn't look so fine.

The three inquired asking
about his health...

"for a name," he humbly said,
"I'd give up all my ivory wealth.

I'm so tired of just being called
grey old me...

there must be a name somewhere...
but oh where would it be?"

Edsel paused only a second in front
of the unusual party of three.

"You can have my name Edsel"
...he laughed out loud with glee.

The elephant was so excited he
jumped up and down.

All over the jungle you could hear
the echoing sound.

The little monkey now with no name
looked up at his happy new friends.

There they were three
smiling faces with huge funny grins.

Today, he thought, has certainly
been fun.

What a good feeling you get inside
when you give to someone.

This smart little monkey would now think up a new name.

The first one he though of was Willie Warren Wayne.

Waving goodbye, he started out for home...

thinking to himself possibly, Jerry John Jerome.